BLACK
RICE

K. M. Kaung

WORDS SOUNDS & IMAGES

Cover design by Todd Hebertson
www.bookcoverart.webs.com

Interior book design and eBook design by Blue Harvest Creative
www.blueharvestcreative.com

Black Rice

Copyright ©2007, 2013 K.M. Kaung
Previously published in *The Northern Virginia Review*, Spring 2007

Published by
WSI (Words Sounds & Images)

ISBN-13: 978 - 0615797526
ISBN-10: 0615797520

Visit the author at:
Website: *www.kmkaung.com*
Blog: *www.kyimaykaung.blogspot.com*
Facebook: *www.facebook.com/kyi.m.kaung*
LinkedIn: *www.linkedin.com/pub/kyi-may-kaung/7/720/26b*

In memory of my late first cousin,
Ko Too, of the very pale skin,
who first told me his story when I was seven.

ALSO BY
K.M. KAUNG

Poetry

Pelted with Petals: The Burmese Poems
Intertext, AK, 1996
ISBN: 0-912767-14-6

Tibetan Tanka
Intertext, AK, 1996
ISBN: 0912767-14-6

Novels

Wolf
Coming Soon

BLACK RICE

My mother Pretty Lady has always called me her little black one. She says my skin is too black. Too, too black. But in spite of that she adopted me and loves me. It's true, she and her brother Uncle Kong have such white skin. You can almost see their blue veins. They act blue-veined too. The endless plays and concerts they go to. The high talk they talk. But my mother, she says it is just because of my jet blackness that she loves me so.

I am the black mascot in their white-skinned family. My eyes at least are slanted like theirs.

The black-skinned little Chinese – Black Rice.

Black Rice, my mother says, is different from the white. White is too delicate, too easily digestible. But the black rice of the hills, it has staying power, it has sticking power. The bricks in the old temples are held together by stucco cement mixed from nothing but lime, sand and boiled sticky rice.

Yet this rice-based cement has held the temples together for hundreds of years. The monk and the nun fortune tellers always say: My name fits my skin color. My skin color matches my name. That is necessary for good luck and for survival. In our country these are necessities, like food and drink, like good health. No one proves that better than the Old Man, Bright Sun himself.

Look how many people have fallen by the wayside. But he goes on, with his well-chosen name, his brilliant *hpon* (my cousin Khine Khine says in English it is "glory" or "soul stuff"), his indestructible *karma*. He always has the good sense to consult with his astrologers before each major move that he makes. And believe me, he's a master chess player, I know. I've played *sitt tu yin* (Burmese chess) with him many times, when we were resisting the Japanese during World War II, fighting the Karen rebels after Independence, setting up the Socialist System Party in 1962. When he went overseas, I've sat outside his hotel bedroom, forty-three times in all. I know the value of loyalty to a great general, of keeping my mouth shut. Only the love of history and drama, not inherited but assimilated from my mother, makes me think I should put this all down now. Then I will hide my diary, or send it secretly to Khine Khine in America; she will know what to do with it. I am growing old and don't care about anything but religion. I don't have children, or a wife, to worry about.

To get back to being well named: My mother always said, black rice is glutinous rice. It's good for breakfast in the morning, with fried fish and shrimp. It'll stay in your stomach the whole day. Indeed, in my fighting days on the front, it kept me alive and feeling strong. The villagers used to boil tightly wrapped banana leaf packets of glutinous rice stuffed with ripe bananas. We soldiers would take them in our knapsacks. It would last us three days. The crust of cooked rice, scraped off the pots and dried in the sun on mats, was, the Japanese used to say, the eternal food. All it needed was to be fried in a little oil. In a crunch, soaked in water, it would keep you alive, your stomach full, to fight another battle, another day.

I always knew I was adopted. My mother told me how much she wanted a child of her own. Her Rh factor and her husband's, my adoptive father's, were not compatible. Hers was negative and my father's positive. She told me, her babies' blood was the same as father's blood and it did not agree with hers. She was allergic to their blood and her body had always repelled and expelled them. She lost ten babies before she gave up trying to conceive. To me, that was a sign from above. She was allergic to her husband's blood and her natural children's, but not to mine. She chose me. I cannot remember her ever saying anything to criticize or hurt me.

She was a storyteller too, my mother, just like Uncle Kong and Aunt Anouk. So I always knew that after her tenth failure at the Dufferin Hospital, she was so sad, she turned her face towards the wall, wishing she were dead, tears streaming from her eyes. Even the jokes of my inebriated father, already tipsy at the afternoon visiting hour, could not make her smile. Her tenth pregnancy had not ended in a miscarriage but in a live birth. To keep the pregnancy, she lay in bed almost all the eight months, hardly moving. On the advice of her doctor, she gave up sex with her husband. She was so proud of carrying to term and of having a live birth. And it was a boy too, she told me. She said his eyes and nose, and ears that stuck out, were just like mine. Just like my father's ears.

She said the worst was when the baby died and her breasts were still full of milk and hurting, but the baby had already been wrapped in a sheet and buried, looking like eighteen inch lengths of sugar cane wrapped in cloth and taken to have the juice squeezed out. She wished her relatives had not told her these things. How her husband, a grown man, had cried holding the stiff bundle in his arms, his face all scrunched up and his feet stumbling over the rocks of the cemetery. When the baby died, her breasts were hard and swollen, like painful water-logged boulders. She might have had a breast abscess, like some other women, had I not come along.

But, she said, I, Black Rice, was a gift straight from heaven. After her tenth failure in the hospital, she was turned towards the wall, crying silently. Even father could not get her to laugh. He tried all his stupid jokes. Then he suddenly turned cold sober again and went to fetch the nurse, who had told him there was an abandoned half-Indian baby in the ward. No one knew who the father was. The mother, Kalama, was a day laborer at one of the construction sites, very pretty and strong, able to climb the bamboo ladders. The struts were tied together with coir rope that creaked under her weight. She carried hundred pound bags of cement, seven bricks at a time carefully stacked up, or a pan of mixed cement on her head to the bricklayers above. At the building project, she was known as the *kalama* (Indian woman) who could shake out a bag of cement as if it were a pillowcase. And the baby was dark but so lovely, a lot of black hair. And he had Chinese eyes. His skin was blue-black, almost purplish black, just like *kauk hnyin nga cheik* or glutinous black rice.

He was healthy and plump.

The nurse was good-hearted and just wanted me to have a home, and Pretty Lady to be happy. She stayed in touch with my family until I was sixteen, when she was lost in the war. She must have convinced my father that a black-skinned Chinese baby like me was good luck. So the nurse bathed me and put on the nicest baby clothes she could find on me. My father had me wrapped in a new diaper and placed me between the wall and my mother.

My mother said she knew at once when I arrived. She had cried herself into a fitful tiredness and was half asleep when the nurse leaned over her and placed me in a bundle against her body. She said I was warm and smelled of coconut oil and sour milk and wet myself at once. My hair was soft down against her cheek. She opened her eyes at once and looked at me. She said she could tell I would grow up to be very good-looking. My skin was dark but my features were like my real father's, whom she thought must have been the Chinese contractor who employed the Indian day laborers.

She kissed me and put her arm around me, so that no one would ever take me away. She was careful not to hold me too closely, in case she smothered me with her large body, or crushed me under her weight. My mother Pretty Lady was big.

My father said when he saw her open her eyes and kiss me, and put her arm around me, he knew she would be all right and that they would take me home. It was true, my skin was a bit too dark, but then so was his. He had checked already that I was as healthy as I looked. He gave my natural birth mother some money, though they could not afford much. He checked on her a few months after my adoption, and he thought my natural father had also given her money, and knew where I was placed.

My mother and he believed, he said, that healthy blood was all that was required. The rest was a matter of environment. And so they took me home and brought me up as their own.

My mother never recovered from her miscarriages. Her monthly seasons reminded her that her body was capable of producing someone of her own blood, and yet she knew it would spit it out again. When my father came home drunk she was angry and made him sleep downstairs in the living room, locking the door to her room while she was inside. It was as if she blamed him for his blood, which did not agree with hers. Once she said to him, "It's good I had those miscarriages. They might have grown up to be drunkards like you."

He hit her then.

In her dressing table drawer under her underwear, she kept a small black book in which she had written all the dates of her slipped babies and the birth and death dates of the one who had died after only one week.

All of them, she said, were boys. Only he had a grave, but it was lost. The river had washed it away.

She never went near the river.

On those days, she would get up early in the morning and say her prayers, sitting on her neatly made bed, bowing down on her pillow, she who never had a shrine room or a Buddha image in her house. Then she'd take her bath and go downstairs, calling the *naan* bread and boiled *vattana pèbyoke* bean vendor to the gate, buying two big stacks of flat bread and a pot full of soft brown boiled beans.

I always knew then that this must be one of the days when her babies had died, just by the quantities that she bought. She bought enough again to feed our whole family. She fed us first, keeping her own food out of sight and saying she didn't feel well; she would eat later. Then when everyone was away at work and at school, she sat down and ate in grief.

I found this out once when I was about ten, had a slight fever and stayed at home. She wanted to pack me off too, so that she would be alone with the ghosts of her dead children, but I really did have a fever. At the same time I wasn't sick enough to be fussed over all the time. Besides, she had already bought the food. She saw to it that I was all right, and that my midday rice gruel was warmed and on the table near my bed.

Then she went downstairs and put her classical Burmese record on the gramophone. She just had one – it was a high woman's voice singing one of the classical odes.

The first line went: "Holding the scroll of the palm leaf script letter to my breast, I . . ."

In the old days people wrote by scratching with a stylus onto a dry palm leaf, a long leaf of the sugar palm, and then rubbing black soot into the scratches. No one could write musical notes in Burma so songs were passed down from teacher to singer to memorize. I thought it strange that my mother chose this song to mourn her children.

I sat at the top of the stairs, hidden behind the fat swell of the rounded teak posts of the banisters and spied on her.

She did nothing but listen to that song, over and over and over, cranking up the gramophone, with the big cornet-shaped loudspeaker turned towards her like an open trumpet flower, a rigid datura,[1] whose seeds can make one forget, forget everything, even one's relatives, they say.

Kill one.

When it lost steam she'd crank it up again angrily, with the volume up so high it shook our small house, and she ate and ate.

Looking down at her from between the banisters, I thought she would burst and all her dead sons but one, my predecessors, would come walking out of her belly.

She did not cry but looked vacantly off into space, seeing nothing, as she broke off raw-edged bits of plate-sized flat *naan* bread. She picked up the mushy boiled beans with the pieces of bread and pushed the food steadily into her mouth with complete indifference, as if eating were a job she hated.

I thought she was doing this to punish herself.

To punish herself for living and finding a living son, while her real sons all died. Eating to feed the spirits of her dead sons.

I knew enough not to come downstairs and shake her out of her trance.

At exactly four in the afternoon, she shook her head vigorously, as if to shake the clinging cobweb memories out – got up, drank a whole pitcher of water, burped loudly, farted, cleared up the table and came upstairs.

She passed close by me, barely touching my head with her hand.

Then she went into her bedroom.

Still stuck to the banisters, I heard the sounds of water, as she flushed the toilet and took a bath, pouring bowlfuls of water out of the filled bath onto herself, she in her wet *longyi*, I'm sure. We Burmese never bathe naked in stagnant water. Then she came out onto the landing, fully dressed in fresh clothes that she must have taken into the bathroom with her.

"Black Rice, how are you feeling? Mother's back," she chirped, as if she had been on a long trip. "Come here, give me a hug."

She pulled me towards her and hugged me tightly.

I felt that but for the enormous folds of her flesh that kept me well insulated, she would have crushed my bones. Her arms felt cool and soft.

"Fever all gone. Back to school tomorrow," she added, feeling my forehead with her open palm.

It felt sticky, even though she had just bathed.

At 5.30 my father came home from the office, already tipsy from his frequent stops at the road-side bars along the way.

Mother went into the kitchen and made an easy dinner for us, swearing as she tried to light the kerosene stove. I scrambled downstairs to help her. She waddled about and soon had our dinner ready. I remember it was quite simple – fried Chinese sausages and a vegetable sour soup with water convolvulus leaves and plain boiled white rice.

It was all right. There was enough of it. Mother never put much energy into making a meal special. That night she ate nothing, having eaten so much already. Father didn't notice and didn't ask. After dinner she gave me a small piece of cake to eat.

Then Father went out, although she protested, to drink with his buddies again.

Mother only tried to shame Father into stopping drinking one last time when I was sixteen, shortly before I ran away to join the Army.

She put on her Sunday clothes which she would have worn to visit friends or if she were the monastery-going type, and went to the bar where she knew he was drinking. To make the shame worse, she wanted me to come with her as I had when I was five years old. But this time I was wary. I didn't want to get mixed up in their affairs. So I refused and stayed home.

She could not make me go to the bar with her and left in a huff.

My father's friends later told me that when Father saw Mother standing silently outside he sobered up at once, after only a few "Why should I go home? These are just women's wiles. I'm not one of those hen-pecked husbands."

His bar mates and he himself must have known, Mother had reached the end of her tether. She was tired of being talked about behind her back as "that fat woman whose husband is an alcoholic."

After about five minutes, Father came out of the bar hanging his head. She walked ahead and he followed, still hanging his head.

That was the only time that he walked behind instead of in front of her.

I remember his delirium tremens were awful. He shook and sweated for weeks, said he saw mosquitoes coming out of his pores. Sometimes at night he'd start to swat and scratch compulsively at his arms. We kept his nails clipped short but it didn't help. His scratched arms bled all over the sheets. When he was uncontrollable like this, my mother would come for me, and together, her considerable weight helping a lot in this, we'd hold him down until he fell asleep.

Sometimes she hummed the ode to calm him.

His sobriety did not last long.

I don't know what triggered his relapse, but one afternoon he just disappeared to the bar again and only came out at 11 p.m., red in the face, his breath stinking of rum and whiskey, his arms around the shoulders of his best friend.

At the bar he had bitten a man's finger. The man got tetanus and threatened to sue him, and would have, except the Japanese came into Burma, making it impossible for anyone to sue anyone, the courts having all been dissolved. All we knew then was that the ones in power were always right.

By then I was mighty tired of fat overeating mother and drunk father.

Once during the war he was drinking the foul local brew at home, because he was too afraid to drink outside: The Japanese would have arrested him. Their justice was of the unyielding type. Mother's eating binges were less, only because there was nothing much to eat. I got fed up and shouted at both of them, "Why the hell did you two adopt me?"

My father, quite drunk, shouted back, "Because she couldn't keep any of her own, of our own, long enough to grow up."

"You know there's a scientific reason," Mother shot back, forgetting you can't reason with a drunk, "your blood never agreed with mine. You *know* it was the Rh factor."

"Right, right, it was my blood that was to blame. I just think it was your womb that was too weak to bear fruit. What's the use of a woman who can't have her husband's children?"

Then turning towards me savagely, "You black son of a bitch! I wish I had not adopted you. You brought bad luck, not good, to our family."

I clenched my fists and got up rapidly from my chair, determined to kill him. "You're the one who's the son of a bitch, married to the bottle!" I laughed derisively.

He lunged at me – too drunk for his left hook to land on my chin.

I dodged and danced around him.

He punched air.

My mother ran between us and hugged me protectively. From behind her huge bulk, looking over her shoulder, I told both of them, "That's it! I'm leaving. I'm damn tired of both of you. I'm not eating your rice a minute more than I need to. I'm joining the Army."

That sobered them both up. They calmed down further when my spinster aunt came in, calling to the neighbors for help. They thought I wouldn't do it.

My mother kept my clothes locked up for a month. I had to go to her for the cabinet keys each time I took a bath or needed a change of clothes. Then I had to return the keys promptly. But she couldn't keep it up for long. I secreted some clothes away each time they were hung on the clothesline to dry, kept them with my friend Sao Sa.

Sa was from the Shan States, and an orphan.

His name meant "Beginning" or pronounced with the other, slightly different "s" sound, "Tease."

He was named after a grand aunt of his who had been born in 1900 and whose name Yarr Sa meant "Century's Start."

It was easy to talk to Sa as he knew what it felt like not to have one's real parents. He was related to one of the powerful Shan *saophas* (tribal chiefs). His mother and father had both died of consumption when they were in their thirties and Sa was quite young. He and his younger sister lived with a rich aunt. Sa and I and my classmates were out of school because under the Japanese everything was closed.

The girls stayed home and helped with the housework – the boys ran loose in the city, only coming back home to eat and sleep.

Politics had gotten a hold of me.

Before the Japanese invasion, even though I was still only in the eighth grade, I would go with my elder cousins and friends and listen to Thakin Aung San[2] talking at the Students Union building on the Rangoon University campus.

He said, "Burma must be an independent nation, not a whoring nation. Burma must stand on its own two feet. Burma must become industrialized."

I was taken by the lean, hungry way he looked, his high cheekbones, the angle of his jaw, the staccato rhythms of his speech, its extreme bluntness.

It was like nothing I had ever heard in Burma before, except for my mother and father uttering home truths.

Everybody else spoke in such veiled, polite, sweet little lies.

Because of politics and the Cause, I thought, I did not need girls or women or a family.

I could be thin and hard and strong like our Great Leader.

Then the Japanese came in an eyeblink.

We heard that Aung San had gone with the Thirty Comrades to Hainan Island and trained to throw out the Enemy. They said on the street that the English had tried to catch him when he stowed away on a boat just before the Japanese invaded. He had disguised himself by shaving his head and wearing yellow robes like a monk, using a set of false teeth that stuck out.

For a while I would look in the mirror every day, push out my even white teeth with my tongue every time I thought about it, so that I would have buck teeth like Aung San in disguise.

During the early years of the Japanese Occupation he formed the Burma Defense Army, and like thousands of other out-of-school young men, I too ran away to join the Army and fight.

It was not as hard as I thought to leave home.

There was just one bad moment when I came downstairs, wearing four layers of shirts and two of pants and saw my mother in her "children dead" daze, not eating now but still gazing out into space, still absently humming that ode that always brought chills to my spine.

I wanted to go back upstairs and hide in my bedroom as if I were ten years old again and had a fever, and was staying home from school just because of it, not because of a war going on.

I knew my friends would say I was a useless sissy who couldn't fight. I should be wearing a woman's flowered *longyi*.

I snuck down into the kitchen and took some dried fish and rice out of the "cat cage" closet with the wire-paneled front, wrapped the food in a sheet of old newspaper and put it all into my Shan bag.

Then trying not to look back at the house with the well and the Green Scent tree near it, I walked to Sao Sa's house to pick up my clothes and run away to the Delta with him to join Aung San and his Army.

The Army wasn't as romantic or glorious as I had imagined.

Many times we were hungry and sick with malaria. The times when we weren't shivering and sweating with the fevers, we were killing people, shooting at them or running way, afraid of being killed ourselves.

The first time I saw a dead man, it was bad, but since it was not someone I knew, I muttered, "Look at that poor bugger," and went on with our forced march to another village in the jungle.

My English shoes that I'd brought with me from home lasted only through one monsoon. At first their bad fit and my splayed feet, used to wearing only thonged slippers, caused blisters to appear on my toes and at the backs of my ankles. My one pair of socks was always wet and smelling like rotten mud and soon torn. Someone stole my extra pair. The bad food was always giving us the runs.

I longed for simple things like a slice of cake from the city or sticking plaster[3] to put on my blistered feet. We passed around a small flat tin of Tiger Balm and put the strong, stinging ointment of eucalyptus on our temples every time the malaria flared up, passing it around among us as if it were as precious as gold. At night I sometimes dreamt of my mother's stacks of *naan* bread. Even boiled beans were a treat.

And so five or six years passed in the jungle.

I lived like all the other soldiers, in dirt and grime and filth.

I didn't read anything because I could not carry books around with me.

In any case, our commander Bright Sun[4] said that reading books was for people who could not act fast.

What would anyone want with weak intellectuals who were forever talking and thinking and arguing this and that and never acting?

In our unit we thought of Bright Sun as a kind of god. We told stories about his drinking and his womanizing, the way he swore with every breath, how compassionate he was towards his *yèbaws* or comrades.

When you are young and have had a bad unhappy childhood, you are looking for gods and heroes.

You have not far to look.

Bright Sun was different from Aung San, I realized this from the start. But I was so taken with him, I did not think deeply enough. And when I did begin to, when I was an old man and Aung San was long dead, and Bright Sun an old, hated man, it was too late.

So then I withdrew into religion. Everyone does.

It's the only safe withdrawal.

Aung San was full of ideas. His speeches were always referring to this or that. It was said he read a lot, drafted his speeches in English. He had a college education. He married a Karen,[5] Christian woman. He was always talking about how all the tribes, all groups in Burma needed to learn how to get on with each other.

On the other hand, Bright Sun knew better how to get on with his soldiers.

He too had gone to Hainan Island, was one of the Thirty Comrades.

I never tired of the story of how, on their way back to Burma, they stopped in Bangkok, and there took the blood oath.

They opened their veins, catching the blood in a silver bowl, mixing their blood together and drinking the mixed blood, vowing to be brothers for life.

When I was young, stories like this carried me along, and made those days and nights in the earthen foxholes, dodging live bullets, more bearable.

Bright Sun was tall, his skin Chinese-yellow, his face flat and broad, his teeth big and even. They said his Chinese name was Shu Maung. He was the son of a postal clerk. I was so caught up in his glory. Even the way he swore seemed to me colorful and frank. In those days we never saw his temper tantrums, which became legendary later on as his power grew. There were hundreds of us runaways who basked in the glamour of these great generals. Aung San we saw from a distance – also General Right Hand[6] and General Magic Wheel Weapon.[7]

But Bright Sun mixed with us. We thought of him as a father. He knew how to gain the loyalty of his chosen sons.

Under Bright Sun's command, I helped finally drive the Japanese out of Burma.

R esistance Day was a glorious day.

My own mother, Pretty Lady, looking pink and plump in the three yards of cloth the army had issued me, placed *aung tha bye* victory leaves in my rifle muzzle during the parade. I saw Aunt Glamis, Uncle Kong's wife, from a distance. She was with someone I didn't know, but she was too far away and I could not hear her. I kept turning around and going "Psst, psst," to attract the attention of other friends and relatives that I saw cheering us on. But I couldn't keep it up for long. My commander did not approve of breaches of discipline like that, of too strong an attachment to family.

And though I wanted to be, I was not under Bright Sun's command for long.

The units got switched around and in 1947 and 1948, we found ourselves fighting every conceivable group.

There were Red Flag Bolsheviks, White Flag Trotskyites, Karen Separatists, China-aligned Maoists and many more groups.

We didn't know what their ideology was. We just called them *yaung zone thu bone* or multicolored insurgents.

By then Aung San was dead, had been assassinated.

Bright Sun called them all the Enemy, out to destroy the nation, by calling for all their little separate nations: How could a country survive fragmented into tiny pieces no bigger than towns? Over the years, Bright Sun defeated almost all these groups: He made them lay down their arms.

He's truly a great leader.

The Karens were the most tenacious of all. They hung on. We fought them for so long. On and on until the eighties. When I think of it now, it seems to me it must be that they were able to hang on like this because of their religion, Baptist Christians that their leaders were. Bo Mya and people like that. All Christians, some converted one or two generations ago by the missionary work of Americans like Adoniram Judson. One of the times I went to America on a military mission to work with the CIA and I saw my cousin Khine Khine, she was working in a motel then and looked so sad.

She said, "Imagine that. Southern Baptist fundamentalist Karens fighting the central government in Burma."

I thought she was being too cynical. She always is.

It is necessary to have a Religion. An army can't fight on swear words and drink alone, though hate is a great thing for winning.

You see how my wisdom all comes too late.

In 1947 we were fighting all along inside the Irrawaddy Delta, the rivers and streams full to overflowing with the monsoon.

I had never seen streams so full before.

They looked as if they would overflow their banks, and that catching the surplus in cups or buckets we would find the true water volume in cubic feet of all that displaced water, the true capacity of all those streams and rivers.

Like one of those asinine arithmetic problems in high school which I could never figure out: One pipe fills a bathtub at ten gallons a minute. Another drains it at five. At the end of eight hours how much water is there left in the bathtub?

I was always tempted to write in my notebook – How the Hell should I know? And who the Hell cares?

S ao Sa and I and the rest of our unit were on a gun boat in the Delta.

It was about 5 p.m. We had just finished our evening meal when the shooting began from the river banks, which had grown narrower and narrower, and closed in around us when we weren't paying attention.

We were in an ambush.

I think it was one of the local pilots who led us into a trap.

I grabbed my rifle and ran out on deck with Sa following close behind. I could see men and young boys on the low branches of the trees overhanging the stream, pointing their rifles at us.

"Ambush! Ambush!" I shouted at the top of my lungs.

Sao Sa and I dove down and took cover behind the iron plates welded to the railings on deck.

Ragged soldiers smelling of sweat, bitter betel spittle and sour rice liquor jumped down onto the deck from the surrounding trees. Bullets whizzed past us, some ricocheting off the metal plates. I saw bare feet rush past and heard groans as people were hit, bangs from exploding shells and thuds as people fell.

More Karen soldiers streamed on board, shouting in a language of which we could not understand a word except, in English – "KNDO! KNDO!" (Karen National Defense Organization) – "Surrender! Surrender!"

The navy officer on duty was shot point blank and killed.

I can still see the red blood blossom slowly expanding outwards on his chest in its bright white uniform, which was stiff and starched.

He died with the pleat in his pants still ironed knife sharp and his black shoes polished to a shine. He was of the old school trained by the British before World War II.

Sao Sa and I flung our rifles down on the bleached grey teak planks of the deck, raised our hands slowly and placed them on the tops of our heads, and waited, wondering what would happen next.

The Karen soldiers prodded us with their rifles in the smalls of our backs, and we were led off, somewhere into the jungle beyond the overfull rivers.

I remember thinking how I wished I still had my English shoes with me as we sloshed through the mud, which made a strong sucking sound every time I drew each foot out of the sludge and left a wet mud line on my calves. At each step my thonged flip flops stuck in the muck. I repeatedly had to stop and pull them out with my hands.

The Karens got impatient and prodded us more sharply, swearing and hitting us, just as we had done with our multicolored prisoners.

The winners take it all, my mother's voice kept saying to me. The winners take it all. The losers standing small.

I was convinced that another of Bright Sun's units would come and rescue us.

Sao Sa had once shown me the Buddhist amulet that he wore around his neck, containing the small piece of the yellow robe of a very holy monk who lived in a cave in the Shan Hills. The little piece of the orange robe coiled up and placed safely in a gold cylinder, shaped like a canister to hold manuscripts.

Sao Sa always kept the amulet around his neck when sleeping, when bathing and when fighting. I suppose also when fucking in the whorehouses to which we sometimes went, into separate curtained bamboo mat-walled "rooms."

Once in Maubin (Ma-oo-bin) I had heard him through the walls, arguing with the prostitute who wouldn't let him do it, unless he took it off first.

I shouted across the top of the flimsily partitioned walls, "Don't, my friend. You'll forget it later. She or her accomplices will rob you of it."

Finally he had come out of the brothel still unsatisfied, because he refused to take off his amulet, and the whore must have him take it off first.

Sao Sa was the butt of many jokes after that.

Now I wondered if his amulet really worked. His amulet that his aunt had saved money for, and had had specially made and placed around his neck. Would my lucky black skin and slanted eyes work also? My mother was too poor and she hadn't known ahead that I was leaving: There was no guardian amulet for me.

The Karen blindfolded us, making some of us use our own handkerchiefs. Then we were marched off, placed in a truck and jounced around for perhaps ten hours. I could hardly tell by the sun swinging around and hitting first my left arm and then my right. Sao Sa managed to stick by me. I felt better that he and I were at least still together.

But we could not talk to each other. When he tried to pinch my hand, to signal something or the other, the soldier who was watching us, sitting on a chair while we sat on the truck bed, hit him sharply.

The folding chair fell over with a clank.

I felt the swish of air from the hand going through the air, heard Sa gasp.

The next moment I was punched sharply on the cheek.

My head swung sideways with a jerk.

Just before I had been blindfolded I had caught a glimpse of the rather good looking though fat man who must be the Karen commander. But I did not recognize him from the rogue's gallery of rebel leaders that our own commander always kept pinned to the mat wall of his headquarters hut.

At the end of the truck trip we were taken to a prison camp. It had nothing but huts for the guards and small bamboo cages, like cages for monkeys or other wild animals.

We were each held captive in a bamboo cage, squatting like cornered animals, only let out once at midday to eat and shit, then locked up again. The cages weren't high enough for us to stand.

The first few days we weren't allowed much exercise time, and almost no bathing time, except when it rained. Then we had nature's warm showers in situ, but even that was not pleasant, for afterwards we remained in our sweaty wet clothes, which were quickly growing mildewed, decaying on us and with us. They fed us a watery rice gruel with salt once a day. I was afraid I would get too weak too quickly.

Holding the squatting posture for hours made my knees tremble and my legs shake when I was finally let out. If the guards saw us sit on our arses, or try to curl up sideways, they opened the bamboo cage door, pulled us out and beat and kicked us.

After eight days we were all let out, and marched off into the rice paddies.

At first I thought we were being marched to another place.

I couldn't tell where we were. All the palm trees and rice fields looked exactly the same. I did not know a word of the Karen language, except *Mo Mo* and *Po Khwa*, which my mother had taught me. She was trying to teach me all the different words for mother and son in as many languages as she knew.

But now the tone of the voices sounded angry, so even if they were saying "mother," they must have been swearing at each other's mothers, and our mothers, I'm sure. As my drunk father used to swear, "Your mother's hubby."

I smiled at the memory of my father, who was too soaked to realize that my mother's hubby was he himself, but this was not the time for smiling.

I saw Sao Sa being marched about ten prisoners ahead of me. Though he was prodded with a bayonet each time he stopped, he still kept slowing his pace slightly. I realized he saw that I was not among the prisoners ahead of him, so he thought I must be behind him.

I saw him gesturing that he needed to shit. One of the Karen soldiers guarding us waved at him: "All right, go ahead, shit. But make it fast."

With the soldier's gun trained on him, I saw Sa go to the edge of the dyke we were walking on, and start to wander off onto a narrower one to the right. The soldier shouted sharply to him to stop.

He turned and walked back a few steps.

I couldn't tell if he saw me or not. I prayed he would do nothing foolish. He turned his back towards us, though the soldier shouted "No!" At least that was one word in Karen that I was beginning to learn.

Sa pulled down his pants and shat.

I and the others behind me kept walking slowly.

I figured out long ago, they didn't like us to stop suddenly. I heard commands shouted from the rear, in the cultivated sing song voice of their commander. I wanted to throw a stone or somehow signal to Sao Sa, but I didn't dare. I knew Sa was waiting for me to pass him to finish doing his thing and stand up. Instead, as I walked past him along the dyke, I leaned over and pulled an imaginary leech off my ankle, and threw it into the fields.

As I passed I smelled his excrement, saw that he really had needed to go.

Sa's stool had the green color and watery consistency of diarrhea.

There were undigested blades of grass in it. I hoped the poor son of a bitch would make it to wherever we were being taken.

Thinking back on it now, I wonder why the obvious did not occur to me. They had too many prisoners to feed, and fighting, or on the run, they could not look after anyone.

They were going to eliminate us.

In a while we came to a stand of trees on a slightly raised bit of land, their roots jutting out above the water line.

It was then, I think, that the truth hit all of us simultaneously.

"They're going to shoot us dead! The Karen sons of bitches are going to shoot us!" one of my comrades cried.

A tall man who had been stumbling along next to Sao Sa panicked and ran off, sloshing through the water in the fields, raising his feet up high, as if in a slow motion film.

They shot him in the back.

His body arched and took a couple more steps on its own, the way headless chickens continue to run around. Then it gyrated and fell into the rice paddy, where the new rice was ten inches high and lush and bright green, with a splash.

The water sprayed out in spokes around him as he fell, glistening in the bright sunlight.

I thought, this is just like a dream, isn't it?

If it isn't so damn real, it's just like a dream.

A bad dream.

Not afraid any more, we were all going to die anyway within minutes, Sao Sa clutched my arm —

"Goodbye, goodbye!" He kept repeating my name, "Black Rice! Black Rice! If I die, tell my aunt. Ask her to forgive me. At least I shall see my father and my mother soon."

"Sa!" I called back, "Don't talk rubbish. You won't die alone. I'm dying with you!"

By now all of us were gibbering last wishes to each other.

A Karen soldier came up near us and slapped Sao Sa and hit me with his rifle butt, hard.

I put my hand up to my jaw, thinking, my teeth must be gone. I tasted my own blood and the jagged edges of cracked teeth.

Sa's hand clutched instinctively at the gold amulet on its chain around his neck, under his buttoned shirt.

The soldier laughed.

He had not seen the chain before but now he knew it was there.

He ripped open Sa's shirt and yanked the chain off. "Burmese soldier! You won't be needing this anymore where you're going."

"Please," Sa begged, getting down on his knees, right there in the muddy water of the rice paddies, "my aunt gave this to me, please."

"Fuck your aunt!"

They had us stand in a line against the trees, almond trees, I think.

I can see them now with their branches growing out horizontally from the main trunk.

Like the tiers of the king's ceremonial white umbrellas.

Yes, almond trees. With their big flat green and gold leaves.

So many times, as children, Sa and I had sat under the almond trees near my house and tried to get at the almonds by smashing the tough little green fruits, shaped like hard eyes and tears, with bricks.

Once I smashed Sa's thumb instead of the almond he was holding edge side up on a brick for me.

He didn't talk to me for a month after that.

The soldiers blindfolded us again.

I stared into Sa's eyes as he was being blindfolded.

I've never seen such sad eyes.

His eyes begged forgiveness of everyone, everything.

Then they were bound with a dirty rag.

My blindfold too smelled of Karen sweat, foul armpit sweat, just like any other sweat.

Fuck war, I thought, fuck everyone.

Fuck politics.

There were about ten of us.

Sao Sa and I were at the end of the line – I was last.

Fuck, I thought, now I have to endure while all my comrades, and especially Sao Sa, are shot.

Why can't they shoot me first? We shouldn't have run away. Why didn't I just stay in Rangoon with my mother and my father?

I thought of attracting attention to myself, by shouting or saying something offensive so that they would shoot me first, but I could think of nothing to say except, fuck.

By then of course it was too late.

It's amazing how short life is, how soon it ends, when you want it to go on.

I was going to get married when the war was over, I told myself.

"But I want to have grandchildren," my mother's voice said to me, very distinctly.

The men standing in line in front of me were shot one by one. At the moment of death, our executioners must have thought that we needed to understand what was going on. Each command of "*Thadi!* Attention!" was in Burmese.

Then the pop and the thuds of bodies falling over, and the smell – of blood mixed with the dank, mildewy smell of water, of urine.

Through it all a light breeze ruffled my hair, the sun shone warmly on my arms, a crow cawed in the distance.

Pop – grunt – groan – thud, pop – thud – groan.

No one pleaded for their lives, no one shouted or cried out.

Then it was Sao Sa's turn.

I could tell, for his hand again clutched my arm, and his voice, shrill as a child's, called out "*Ah May yé kè par!* Mother, save me!"

"I am Shan!" he cried, "I'm not even Burmese. This has nothing to do with me."

But it was long past logic and reasoning.

Someone shouted back, "Mother-fucking lying Burman – with a Buddhist amulet around his neck. Do you expect us to believe that?"

Then, pop, groan, and Sa's hand went loose, lost its grip and slid off my arm.

My groin felt warm and sticky.

I must have wet myself.

My belly felt empty.

My heart was pounding in my chest.

The blood must have risen to my head. I never felt so lucid in my life. Something dripped onto my left foot, flowing in a trickle over it.

Then something soft and warm, the size of a small sand bag, fell onto it.

The top of my foot felt sticky. I thought I felt hair.

My turn came in a second — an eternity.

Awkatha, Awkatha, Awkatha, I repeated desperately in my head – the Gem of the Buddha, the Gem of the Dharma, the Gem of the Sangha.

I seek Refuge in The Three Jewels.

A small cold circular thing was pressed against my temple.

I smelled stale sweat on khaki, stale fermented palm liquor on the breath, heard more swearing.

Whatever it was, a pistol, a revolver, it jammed.

After that I remembered nothing. I must have fainted.

I came to in a hut with the soft-spoken Karen commander sponging my naked body with a damp rag.

I tried to get up. I wanted to know what had happened to my friends.

"Mother-fucker, why didn't you kill me too," I groaned.

But he shushed me, told me to rest. I would be safe with him. He understood and could speak Burmese well, he told me. He just did not want to speak it as a matter of principle. And also, he continued, as a matter of security, we were to speak to each other in English. Did I speak English? Well, of course I must. Went to a high school in Rangoon, probably. Even speaking to him in English, I wouldn't be completely safe. Still, a better chance that the lower class, uneducated foot soldiers wouldn't understand us. Yes, stay with him as his personal servant. I would be safe, at least for a while.

I stayed with the Karen commander in a village whose name I cannot speak of, for several months, while the Karen uprising swirled around us.

There were doubtless people, old men and women and children in the village, who were all collectively watching me and my movements. I couldn't run away because I knew I was in Karen territory. I realized I wouldn't get very far without being recaptured. Besides, not knowing exactly where I was, except that I was somewhere in the vast Irrawaddy Delta region, I really did not know which direction to run.

Every day, I cooked the commander's food for him.

He liked *nga pi yay cho or nga pi lain mar* – sweet or "good" fish sauce carefully dressed with pounded chilies, garlic and dried shrimp, served with fresh boiled jungle greens and fried fish.

In the mornings after a breakfast of glutinous rice, he went off to fight his War.

While he was gone, in the daytime I washed his clothes, spread them out on the bushes to dry and tended a small vegetable patch. I grew rabbit greens, eggplant and water spinach. My hot chilies, sprouted from seed, did quite well. In the evening I pulled buckets of water up from the well for his bath, served the evening meal. I fanned the mosquitoes off him as he sat on the front steps of the bamboo hut, sang the only stanza of my mother's favorite ode that I remembered to him.

"Holding the bud of the palm leaf script letter to my breast."

Every night while I was fanning him and singing, the other Karen soldiers and officers, all slightly drunk, would come up to him, start talking to him excitedly in their own language.

He told me in English that what they wanted was to take me away to kill me. "Give us the black-skinned Burmese boy with the slanty eyes," they said, "we need to shoot him. Haven't shot enough Burmese for today. Makes our trigger fingers itchy."

Every night I heard how he soothed them, telling them jokes, placating them in one way or the other, until they went off guffawing into the night.

Every day I started to worry that a stray bullet or an intended one would hit my commander and that they'd bring him back dead on a stretcher. His rivals might plot to kill him or he might be poisoned by the Burmese.

I think he realized this too and while I sang the ode, he would look at me with sad blurry eyes.

Once I asked him why he had saved me.

"Revolver ran out of bullets."

"You could have gotten a gun off any of the soldiers."

"More accurately, the gun jammed."

"You could have had me beaten or starved to death."

"All right then, all right – Black Rice, if you must hear it! I loved your black-skinned face. I thought if the gun jammed, it must mean that God did not want you to die."

After that I stopped asking him why he had spared me.

As I sang to him at night, it seemed to me that he grew bleaker and older as the year wore on. He didn't say anymore as he used to in the early days, "We're going to beat you damned Burmans.[8] Rangoon is going to fall in a couple of days. Just you wait and see." Instead, now he often said, "We Karens are descended from the lost tribes of Israel. We're destined to wander in the Wilderness forever."

I thought he was just getting dejected because they were losing – but could not be sure exactly how the civil war was playing out.

No one was telling me anything.

One night he said, "Oh, stop singing that stupid song. In future we won't sit on the veranda after dinner any more. You don't need to fan me and sing to me anymore."

So I stopped and went to bed early, thinking about the war, thinking about my father and my mother, thinking about the future of my Country.

But my thinking always ran in circles because I knew nothing except that fighting and having my friends killed, especially Sao Sa, had been no fun.

No fun at all.

What would I tell his aunt and his sister when it was all over?

One dark night, when the moon was waning, the rain was falling and the frogs were making strange clicking sounds, impatient for the full moon to start mating, the commander came into my room, gave me some money, a spare set of clothes and a map, sketched on a page torn out of a notebook.

He sat down cross-legged with me on the floor, and spreading the sheet of paper on the worn planks by the light of a candle, made sure I knew where I was, and the orientation of the free-hand map.

"You are here," he stabbed with his index finger, as I held the candle up to the map.

N-S, E-W – he wrote rapidly in a cross shape on the top right hand corner.

A drop of wax from the candle fell on the map.

I pulled it away sharply.

"Be careful, now, don't let the thing catch fire. Keep it in a safe place."

He showed me how to roll it up tightly like a cigarette, and hide it in the small narrow pocket made by the torn front hem of my shirt. How to tuck my shirt in under my *longyi*.

He went into the kitchen and came back with two big packets of food wrapped in banana leaves and tied together with a vine.

"Go now," he ordered gruffly, "here is rice and dried fish," slinging the two rice packets around my neck.

They hung in front of my chest like *nwa khalauk* wooden bells on a cow's neck.

"How can I thank you for saving my life," I cried out, getting down on my knees and bowing down to him in the Buddhist way, as if saying goodbye to my father or to a beloved elder brother.

Saying goodbye to Sao Sa.

The two rice packets hit the floor as I bowed down, till my forehead, both my palms and my elbows were all touching the floor.

"No need, no need," he said, pulling me up, "no need for one human being to bow down to another."

"I owe my life to you."

He dipped his finger into the bowl of cold tea standing on the low table, made the sign of the cross on my forehead, murmuring, "May God keep you my son."

"Please tell me," I rushed on, standing up, "what I can do for you, in gratitude. For this eternal debt. If ever you come to Rangoon, my home. If ever."

He laughed harshly. "As if we could just visit each other and have afternoon tea, with cucumber sandwiches, huh? With pickled tea salad. A bite of ginger salad. That's a luxury for lesser, civilian mortals. No need to worry – this time next year, I'll be dead and gone. Bones decayed probably. Eels coming out of my eye sockets."

"Don't talk like that," I protested, "God has kept you so far. He'll keep you yet."

"Ha! Did a prayer ever stop a bullet? Better get going my friend."

He pushed me out the back door, which squeaked as it swung open.

"Please," I pleaded, looking backwards at him, "Please, say how I am to repay you."

"Well," he said, his tongue seeming to flag in his mouth, swelling and filling it, making him lisp. "First things first. Never mention my name to another human being."

I nodded in the darkness. "Yes, yes, of course."

"Second, easy enough," he continued, "Small debt. Not deep into your pockets. Someday, any day, save a life for me," he hissed. "Save a life and send the merit to me. God knows I will need all I can get."

END NOTES

1 - Angel's trumpet, every part of which is deadly poisonous.

2 - Before Aung San became Bogyoke or General Aung San, he was a member of the Thakin Group, which set themselves up as rivals to the British colonialists who called themselves "thakin" or saviors.

3 - Bandaid

4 - Ne Win

5 - Karen or Kayin, an ethnic group.

6 - Bo Let Ya

7 - Bo Set Kya

8 - The collective racial term Burmese is composed of various ethnic groups such as Burmans, Shan, Karen, Kachin, Chin, Pao, Wa etc.

AUTHOR'S NOTE & ACKNOWLEDGEMENTS

Ko Too, my elder cousin, first told me his story when I was seven, and had just come home to Burma from England with my parents and siblings. He may have been about eighteen or twenty at that time, but like that side of the family, he told stories with great aplomb.

He is the first person I should thank.

Todd Heberston designed the cover and the bamboo fleuron. The creative team at Blue Harvest Creative carried out the formatting and support services. Thank you.

Originally, it was not a free standing novella but was part of an autobiographical novel that I wrote in the late nineties, while my mother and other relatives were still alive.

This novel was workshopped in James Rahn's Rittenhouse Writers' Group in Philadelphia.

In Washington DC an African-American friend persuaded me to send it out again, and it was published in a print version of *The Northern Virginia Review*, Spring 2007.

That edition was edited by Dorothy Seyler.

I have since reworked it a bit more and edited it myself.

About seven years ago, a former Karen rebel leader told me he knew Ko Too and also mentioned the name of the Karen officer who saved him. But I promptly forgot the name again, as I am primarily a writer of fiction.

I think it is a good time for *Black Rice* to be published as the civil war with the Karen has gone on for over sixty years, and only now is there a glimmer of hope of Peace, but there are still all sorts of conflicts still on-going in Burma.

www.ingramcontent.com/pod-product-compliance
Lightning Source LLC
Chambersburg PA
CBHW070355130626
46556CB00007B/3180